BACK ON
TRACK

BY JAKE MADDOX

text by
Joelle Wisler

STONE ARCH BOOKS
a capstone imprint

Jake Maddox JV Girls books are published by
Stone Arch Books
a Capstone imprint
1710 Roe Crest Drive
North Mankato, Minnesota 56003

www.mycapstone.com

Cataloging-in-Publication Data is available on the Library of Congress website.
ISBN: 978-1-4965-7536-4 (library binding)
ISBN: 978-1-4965-7538-8 (paperback)
ISBN: 978-1-4965-7546-3 (eBook PDF)

Summary: Addison Jones is joining the track team—even though her mom said no.
Addison has come up with a risky plan to compete, but soon she's torn between her
love of sprinting relay races and the guilt over lying to her mom. How can Addison
pursue her running passion?

Designer: Tracy McCabe
Media Researcher: Tracy Cummins

Image Credits:
Shutterstock: Annette Shaff, Design Element, ROMSVETNIK, Cover

Printed and bound in China.
000970

TABLE OF CONTENTS

CHAPTER 1

FLYING FEET

Twelve-year-old Addison Jones pumped her arms and legs as fast as they would go. She flew down the dirt track. Her worn-out running shoes scraped against the rocky ground, driving her forward. She loved how her body felt as if it was made out of fire.

Addison rounded the final corner and poured every last bit of energy into her legs. She could taste the dust from the track inside her mouth. Her lungs ached with each big breath, but she kept pushing.

She wasn't going to let up until the race was completely over.

The other runners were so far behind her that Addison couldn't even hear the slap of their feet anymore. She felt free and alive. She'd had no idea running could be like that.

The rest of Addison's PE class burst into cheers as she slid over the finish line in first place. Their teacher, Ms. Barnes, gave Addison a high five.

"Awesome race, Addison," Ms. Barnes said, her eyebrows raised with surprise.

Addison felt a shiver of joy as she watched the other girls starting to cross the finish line. She'd been so *fast*.

"Thanks!" Addison managed to reply between big, tired breaths. She bent over and put her hands on her knees. Sweat poured down her face and plopped onto her shoes in dark splotches.

Addison's friend Sofia jogged past. She was the last one to finish the race. Sofia hated running.

Sofia hates anything that isn't reading books with magical creatures in them, Addison thought with a smile.

The two friends were as different as could be. Addison was quiet and shy. Sofia could make friends with anyone, anywhere. When she didn't have her face buried in a book, that was.

The two girls had been inseparable since first grade. One day, Sofia had sat next to Addison at lunch and declared they were best friends forever. That was all it took.

"Wow, Addie, you were so fast. I think you almost lapped me!" Sofia said.

Sofia flipped back her long, jet-black hair. It was pulled back into a slick ponytail. She looked completely relaxed and calm. Not at all like she'd just finished running a 400-meter race.

"It was only one lap!" Addison said, laughing. She knew her own face was red and shiny. Sweat was still dripping down her forehead.

But Addison didn't care. Running as fast as she could had been the most fun she'd had in a long time.

FWEET!

Ms. Barnes blew her whistle. It was the signal for all the kids in PE to head back to the school. Sofia and Addison started walking.

Ms. Barnes came up beside Addison. "You know, Addison, we could really use your speed on the track and field team," she said. "Have you thought about joining?"

Addison wasn't sure how to respond. She was happy that Ms. Barnes had noticed her. But there was also a sinking feeling in her stomach. She couldn't join the track team.

Every night, she had to watch her little brother after school while her mom worked the late shift at a nursing home. She couldn't be on the track team at the same time that she was making dinner and putting Charlie to bed.

"Uh, maybe," Addison said finally.

It didn't seem like Ms. Barnes noticed the pause. "Tryouts are right after school," she said. "Will I see you there?"

"I'll try," Addison said, her voice filled with false cheer. But she wouldn't try. She couldn't.

Addison felt the hot prick of tears in her eyes. She was surprised. She hadn't even known that she loved to run.

Swiping a hand over her face, Addison yelled, "Come on, Sofia! Let's race!"

Addison didn't want to cry in front of her teacher. Or anyone. She didn't want people feeling sorry for her. She loved Charlie, and her mom needed her. It was as simple as that.

She sprinted toward the gym room door.

"Hey, wait up!" Sofia shouted.

As she ran, Addison's tears dried up. She slammed into the door first, beating Sofia by a full two seconds. The other girl jogged up, laughing.

9

The rest of the school day went by in a blur of math equations and state capitals. Addison didn't really have time to think about how much she'd loved running the race. And she tried extra hard to stop thinking about trying out for the track team.

* * *

Every day after school, Addison picked up Charlie from kindergarten. That day, she looked inside as Charlie got ready to go. The classroom was loud and colorful. The little kids were all chatting and giggling. They dropped piles of artwork as they tried to put their wiggling arms into jackets.

"Addie!" Charlie shouted. His face lit up when he saw his big sister. He had a smudge of pink paint on his cheek, and his hair was messy.

Addison smiled. Seeing Charlie made her feel just a little better about missing the track tryouts.

"Hey, munchkin," Addison said. She helped her brother lift up his bulging backpack. "Whoa, what do you have in here, rocks?"

"Yeah!" Charlie said. "We painted rocks today, and I got to be the special helper and . . ."

Addison tried to pay attention to her brother's stories as they walked home. They lived eight blocks from school, and Charlie usually talked the entire way.

As they passed the middle school track, Addison saw the runners walking onto the field. Ms. Barnes was there with a clipboard and stopwatch. Addison also spotted Brie, Carly, and Ginny. They were some of the girls she had raced in PE.

The girls were all wearing running shoes in rainbow colors. The bright oranges and pinks and greens stood out against the sand-colored track. The sun went behind a cloud just as Addison felt a prick of jealousy land in her belly.

She wished she was out there too. She wished she had brand-new running shoes. She would lace them up strong and tight.

Addison imagined herself rushing down the track during a meet. She could hear the stands of fans cheering wildly. And she could feel exactly how the finish-line tape would feel as she broke through it.

The hardest part was that Addison knew she was faster than Brie, Carly, *and* Ginny. But that didn't matter.

She looked down at Charlie. He was talking about who he'd sat next to at lunch and reporting that they'd played kitties again at recess. Addison gave his shoulder a little squeeze. The two of them continued on toward home.

I have to put track out of my mind for good, Addison thought. *I'm not a baby. I can get over it.*

Then it hit her.

I'm not a baby, she realized. *I'm a* babysitter.

And if she could find a different babysitter for Charlie, she could join the track team.

She'd just have to convince her mom to go along with it.

CHAPTER 2

DISAPPOINTMENT

That night, Addison reheated leftover macaroni and cheese in the microwave. Charlie sat at the counter, drawing blue and green dinosaurs.

"Here you go, buddy," she said. She placed the steaming plate down in front of her little brother.

"Mac and cheese again?" he said.

Addison had to admit, the sticky noodles didn't look very delicious. "Yes, again," she told Charlie. "It's either this or canned soup, and I know how much you love that."

Charlie made gagging sounds.

"That's what I thought," said Addison.

She took her own plate and sat at the counter next to him. Her math homework was spread out in front of her like a fan.

"Maybe you should learn how to cook some other stuff?" Charlie looked at her hopefully.

Addison stabbed a gooey noodle. "Yeah, I probably should," she said.

"Like hamburgers or spaghetti or pizza or chocolate-covered strawberries!" Charlie said as he twirled his food around on his plate. Addison grinned. Charlie did love strawberries.

* * *

After reading four picture books to Charlie and promising that she would learn how to make chocolate-covered strawberries, Addison said good night. Then she quietly left his room.

Addison went into the living room and started tidying up. When she was done with that, she made sure the kitchen was sparkling clean. She wanted Mom to be in a good mood when she told her about the plan to join the track team.

Addison was sitting at the counter, finishing her homework, when her mom walked in the door. Grocery bags hung from both of Mom's arms. She had dark circles under her eyes.

Mom set the bags down with a big sigh. "Hey, Addie. Is Charlie asleep?" she asked. She came over and kissed Addison on the forehead. She looked exhausted, and Addison felt a pinch of guilt.

"Yep," Addison said. She jumped off the counter stool and put a plate of macaroni and cheese into the microwave. "How was your day, Mom?"

"Oh, you know, long and tiring," Mom replied as she sat down at the counter.

Addison knew how hard her mom worked. She and Charlie never went without anything. They always had clean clothes, even if they were secondhand. They always had full bellies, even if it was just cheese sandwiches and tomato soup.

The evening shift at the nursing home meant her mom made more money. She'd promised Addison that babysitting Charlie after school would be temporary—a month at the most.

But one month turned into two. Now it had been an entire year.

Addison looked at Charlie's drawings that hung on the refrigerator. She loved her brother, and she didn't mind watching him. She just wanted to go to Sofia's house after school every once in a while. Or join the track team. Or just be a kid.

She thought back to how she'd felt running around the track. How her body had felt as if it was *meant* to run. How she had felt as if she were flying.

She needed to find the courage to ask her mom about track.

"We ran a race today in PE," Addison started. She took a deep breath and began to spin a pencil around her fingers. Addison always fidgeted when she was nervous. "I beat everyone by, like, a mile."

"That's great," Mom murmured. She was flipping through a magazine. Addison wasn't sure her mom was even listening to her.

"Afterward, Ms. Barnes said she'd love to have me on the track team," Addison went on. "Tryouts were today. But I couldn't go. Because of Charlie."

At that, her mom looked up. There was sadness in her eyes. "I'm sorry, Addie," Mom said. "You know I need you to babysit him after school."

"What about Mrs. Davis?" Addison asked, rushing the words out. "She used to babysit me when I was little, right?"

Mrs. Davis lived down the block. She had a cute dog that Addison had loved to play with.

"Yes," Mom replied. "It's just that Mrs. Davis charges money. I'm working hard so we can get ahead. I don't have the money to pay Mrs. Davis."

Addison's heart sunk. "Oh," she said quietly. "I didn't know she charged."

She felt her face flush. *Of course Mrs. Davis charges money for babysitting*, she told herself. *Why hadn't I thought of that?*

"I'm really sorry, Addie," Mom said.

"It's OK," Addison said quickly. She felt tears coming for the second time that day. "I'd probably hate being on the track team anyway."

Before her mom could say anything else, Addison stacked up her homework and hurried to her room.

CHAPTER 3

RUNNING FOR FUN

The next day was another running lesson in PE for the Franklin Bulldogs middle schoolers. At first, Addison's legs felt sore from the race the day before. As she took long strides, though, her muscles loosened. Soon she was passing all of the other kids during their warm-up laps.

But with each step, she felt more disappointed. It was fun to run. But she would never be able to join the track team. She could never run a *real* race.

"Show-off!" Sofia yelled, laughing as Addison lapped her.

Addison didn't slow down. She kept pumping her legs and arms. She imagined she was a cheetah. A gazelle.

Ms. Barnes tweeted her whistle. "All right, everyone. Now that you're loose, let's do some sprinting drills," she told them. "Run as fast as you possibly can for one hundred meters. Then walk for fifty, and then sprint again. Let's go!"

Addison flew around the track during the sprints. The wind blew through her hair. Even in her worn-out shoes, she was faster than all the girls. *And* the boys.

"This will be the last one hundred-meter sprint!" Ms. Barnes shouted.

Addison let her legs do what they wanted to do. She ran as fast as she could. Her legs burned with the effort, but she didn't let up until she crossed the mark on the track.

Once everyone had finished, the class gathered over on the grass around their teacher.

"Next we're going to work on some different conditioning exercises," Ms. Barnes said. "These will help strengthen your muscles. Then you can run even faster."

Addison's class stood in a line while Ms. Barnes called out different exercises for them to do.

"Lunges!" she yelled, and they all lunged.

"Jumping jacks!" she yelled, and they all jumped.

"Squats!" she yelled, and they all squatted.

It was tiring. By the time they were done, Addison was covered in sweat. She and Sofia fell to the ground.

"That was so much fun," Addison said, smiling. Her body felt like a wet noodle.

"Fun? You have to be kidding me," Sofia said. "That was more like torture."

"I loved it," Addison said, and she meant it. The exercises had been hard, but she enjoyed the way it felt to push herself to the edge.

And if doing the exercises could make her run even faster? That was just a bonus.

Sofia shook her head. "You are one weird girl, Addison Jones."

Addison laughed. "I might be weird, but at least I'm *fast*."

"You know, you really are so much faster than everyone out here," Sofia said. She rolled over and tugged on a blade of grass. "It's so obvious you love running. You need to join the track team."

"I can't," Addison said. "You know that my mom needs me to watch Charlie."

"Maybe I could help somehow," Sofia said. She raised an eyebrow. She always made that face when she was coming up with a plan.

"I don't think you can," Addison said. "But don't worry about it. It's my problem, not yours."

The rest of the class went by in a flurry of kicked-up dirt. Addison ran until sweat was dripping down her back.

If PE was the only chance she'd get to run, she was going to give it her all.

By the time the period was over, Addison's legs were shaky and weak. She could barely make it up the stairs to the locker room.

Addison and Sofia changed and gathered their backpacks. They were about to head to algebra when Ms. Barnes walked over.

"Hey, Addison, can I talk to you for a moment?" Ms. Barnes asked.

Sofia nudged Addison before waving goodbye. Addison turned back toward the teacher. "What's up, Ms. Barnes?"

"We missed you at track tryouts last night," Ms. Barnes said.

"I know," Addison said. She shifted her bag. "I couldn't make it."

"I'd really love to see you out there," Ms. Barnes said. "Even though you missed the tryouts, you can still join the team. What I saw today convinced me."

"Really? That's so cool. Thank you," Addison said happily. Then she thought of her mom's tired face. "But I'm just too busy with . . . other stuff."

She didn't want to admit to Ms. Barnes that she couldn't join track because she had to watch her brother. Ms. Barnes would just ask why they couldn't get a babysitter. Addison would be forced to tell her about her family's money problems.

"Well, promise me you'll at least think about it," Ms. Barnes said. "Our first practice is tomorrow after school. If you decide to come, you just need to bring the activity fee."

"OK," Addison said, trying to sound calm.

"I hope you'll come," Ms. Barnes said. "See you tomorrow." She smiled and went back into her office.

Addison stood in the hallway, staring down at her dirty shoes. *What am I going to do now?* she thought.

Addison kept thinking as she walked toward her next class. *Being on the track team would be a dream come true,* she told herself. *There has to be a way to join.*

She had a little bit of birthday money from her grandparents. She had it stashed in her jewelry box at home. She'd been saving it, but it would probably be enough for the activity fee.

Charlie's chubby face, covered in pink paint, swam into her mind. But what would she do about Charlie?

Addison slid into her seat in algebra. Next to her, Sofia had one eyebrow raised again.

"I've been thinking," Sofia said. "I have an idea for solving your track problem."

"Yeah?" Addison said, smiling. For the first time, she felt really hopeful. The two girls ducked their heads together and started whispering.

CHAPTER 4

THE PRACTICE PLAN

The next day after school, Addison, Sofia, and Charlie walked over to a small playground. It stood right by the middle school track.

Addison sat in the grass as she laced up her scuffed-up running shoes. They pinched her toes a bit, but she wouldn't be asking her mom for a new pair.

After all, her mom didn't even know that she was joining the Bulldogs track team.

The two friends had figured the entire plan out together. Sofia was going to watch Charlie at the playground during practice. That part had been her idea. Addison could pay the track team activity fee with her birthday money. And with Sofia looking after Charlie, she wouldn't have to worry about her brother.

Addison stood up and placed her fingers on Charlie's chin so he would look her in the eyes. "Listen to Sofia, OK, pip-squeak?"

He brushed her hand away. "I will, I will," Charlie said. "I'm not a baby, you know."

"I know," said Addison. "And no matter what, remember that you can't tell Mom."

Charlie nodded seriously.

"Are you sure you're OK with this?" Addison asked her friend.

Sofia gave Addison a quick hug. "You'll just have to get me front row tickets when you make it to the Olympics."

"Deal!" Addison said.

The two girls grinned at each other. Addison was so excited to run. She was almost able to ignore the guilty feeling in the back of her mind.

As Addison jogged toward the track, she glanced back at Sofia and Charlie. Sofia sat on a wooden bench, already deep into her book. Charlie was climbing up the playground slide.

This might actually work, Addison thought as she stepped onto the track.

"Addison!" Ms. Barnes exclaimed. "I'm so happy to see you. Welcome to the team! You're just in time for our warm-up."

Addison smiled at the coach and then joined the large group of kids standing near the starting line. A couple of the girls looked over at her.

Brie, a girl in her PE class with bright orange hair, came to her side. "Hey, Addison!" Brie said. "Are you joining track?"

Addison nodded.

Brie grinned. "Cool! I really hope I get to be in a relay race with you. You're so fast!"

Addison laughed and said, "Thanks!"

"OK," Ms. Barnes called to the group. "Time to jog. Half a mile. That's two times around the track. Go slowly at first so your muscles can gently warm up."

The team started jogging. After the first lap, Addison felt her muscles begin to loosen.

Her feet hit against the rough track. She tried to ignore the fact that she could feel each pebble through the thin soles of her shoes. Her toes dug into the ends with every step.

Addison couldn't help but glance over at Brie's bright yellow shoes. She felt jealous of the new, colorful footwear. Addison would've even settled for older ones that were the right size.

When they finished the laps, the group of kids circled around Ms. Barnes and the other track coaches.

"We're going to break you into groups of four," Ms. Barnes told them. "Each group will work on a different track skill."

She went on to explain the activities. There would be long distance running, triple jumping, and hurdling, along with a lot of other events. When she was done, the coaches organized the kids into groups. Addison was in one with Brie, Ginny, and Laura.

"You four are going to work on sprinting," Ms. Barnes told them. "You're all really fast."

A sprinter, Addison thought with a smile. She liked the sound of that.

"Let's try a relay race to start," Ms. Barnes said. She picked up a hollow yellow stick and tossed it between her hands.

Addison had seen relay races before on TV. The runners each ran part of the race. Those parts were called legs. When one person was done with her leg, she passed a stick to the next runner.

"This is a baton," their coach continued, holding up the yellow stick. "You'll need to hand it off to the next runner in the exchange zone. That's an area on the track that's twenty meters long. If you don't hand it off in time, the whole team is disqualified."

Ginny raised her hand. "What happens if we drop it?" she asked.

"Dropping the baton won't automatically disqualify the team, but you may end up breaking another rule, like interfering with other runners. And it *will* slow you down," Ms. Barnes replied. "It'll make it nearly impossible to win."

Addison gulped. She hoped she would never drop the baton.

"First, we'll practice the fastest way to pass the baton," Ms. Barnes said. "The best relay teams can hand it off smoothly and quickly so you don't lose any time."

The coach lined the girls up in the order they would be running. Ms. Barnes told Addison that she would be the team's anchor. That meant she'd run the last leg of the race.

Addison smiled. She was excited to be the one who would cross the finish line. She couldn't wait to experience the feeling of breaking the tape.

And she just knew she would be breaking the tape.

CHAPTER 5

RELAY RACE

For most of track practice, Addison, Brie, Ginny, and Laura worked on passing the baton between them. They dropped it a lot. The other girls giggled every time the plastic tube clattered to the ground.

Addison huffed out a frustrated sigh as she got back into position to practice the handoff. She wanted to get it right. She had risked a lot just to be on the team. She wanted everyone to take practice as seriously as she was.

"Make sure your teammate has a good grip on the baton before you let it go!" Ms. Barnes called to them. "Keep your hand on the lower half so the next runner can easily grab the top."

The four sprinters kept practicing. Eventually, they figured out how fast they needed to run to smoothly pass the baton inside the exchange zone. They started to slap the baton into each other's palms with a loud *smack*!

The girls were too focused to laugh at their mistakes now. They started to work as a real team.

After a near-perfect handoff between each girl, Ms. Barnes nodded. "I think you're ready to run the full relay race," she said. "Just like you'll do at the first track meet a week from Saturday."

Oh no, Addison thought. Her stomach started to hurt. *I didn't think about meets being on Saturdays!*

Her mom had Saturdays off. Addison wouldn't have to worry about Charlie. But her mom would definitely notice if she was gone for half the day.

Addison was going to have to figure out something to tell her.

The lies were starting to build. Addison didn't want to lie. She just didn't know what else to do. She had to run.

Addison looked over at the playground. She could see Charlie swinging on the swings. Sofia was pushing him with one hand. She was reading a book with the other. They both looked perfectly happy.

One day at a time, Addison thought. She'd deal with the track meet later.

The girls lined up in their race order. They would be practicing the 4x400-meter relay. Each girl would run around the track one time. Then they would pass the baton to the next runner.

Ginny was first, because she was the second fastest. She would pass to Laura, and then Laura would pass to Brie. She would do the final handoff to Addison, who was the fastest of the four.

And Addison planned on running like the wind.

Ms. Barnes held her stopwatch. Ginny was stooped low in her starting position.

"On your mark, get set, go!" Ms. Barnes shouted.

Ginny took off, kicking up dirt with her bright purple running shoes. Addison and the other girls cheered as she ran.

As each girl spun around the track, Addison waited for her turn. Each handoff went just as they'd practiced.

Brie started off strong and flew around the first corner. But Addison wondered if Brie was going too fast at the beginning. If she didn't save some energy, she wouldn't be able to finish strong. It was hard to learn to rely on other runners.

Finally, Brie started to come down the final stretch. She had lost some speed, but she was still giving it her all.

While Addison waited, her right leg bounced up and down. Brie was twenty meters away now. Addison could feel her body tense. Brie got closer and closer. Just when she was the right distance away, Addison started to jog.

She reached her arm back to receive the baton. Brie reached forward.

Slap! The baton hit Addison's hand. It was slippery with sweat.

For one terrifying moment, Addison thought she might drop it. She gripped her fingers around the baton and hung on. Then she tucked it close to her body and ran.

Show them what you've got, she thought. Her legs responded to the command. An extra surge of energy moved her forward. She dashed around the first corner and down the straightaway.

Through the rush of wind in Addison's ears, she could hear the other girls cheering her on. That made her run faster.

When Addison rounded the last corner, her mind cleared. She tried not to think about Charlie, her mom, or the guilt she felt.

Instead, she concentrated on moving her body in perfect symmetry. Arms up and down. Legs up and down. Eyes ahead. Fingers squeezing the baton.

She dashed across the finish line, and the other girls ran around her. They patted her back, talking all at once.

"Wow, that was amazing!" Brie said.

"You ran so fast!" Ginny shouted.

"I think we're going to win every single race!" Laura added with a laugh.

Addison's muscles felt as if they were going to melt. Her heart beat fast. And when she looked up, Ms. Barnes was grinning at her.

"Great run, Addison!" Ms. Barnes said. "You finished in under sixty-five seconds. Some high school runners can't even get that kind of time."

Addison smiled and hugged her teammates. Joining track—even though it wasn't easy—was worth it.

CHAPTER 6

THE PLAN GOES WRONG

Addison loved track. After a week of practice, she could already feel herself becoming stronger and faster. She knew she was ready for the first track meet on Saturday. She was going to run the 100- and 200-meter races and the 4x400 relay race. Addison hoped to get all first-place medals.

And off the field, things were going well too. Sofia and Charlie were getting along great. Addison's mom didn't suspect a thing.

Everything was going just as planned.

Then, the day before the track meet, disaster struck. Sofia wasn't at school.

Addison sat in homeroom. Her knee bounced as she kept glancing toward the door, waiting to see Sofia walk in. But the door didn't open. So at the end of the period, Addison stopped at Mr. Carlton's desk.

"What can I do for you, Addison?" Mr. Carlton asked.

"Do you know where Sofia is?" she asked. "We were . . . um . . . supposed to work on a project together today." *That's not technically a lie,* she thought.

"Let me see," Mr. Carlton said. He dug into a big pile of papers on his desk. "I think I had a message about her here somewhere."

Addison gripped her backpack straps as she waited. Maybe Sofia had gotten so caught up in one of her books that she had lost track of time. Maybe she was just late.

Addison hoped that was what had happened. Because if Sofia didn't come to school, Addison wouldn't be able to go to practice. The first meet was tomorrow. She didn't want to let her team down.

"I found it!" Mr. Carlton exclaimed. He pushed his smudged glasses up on his nose and peered at the note. "It says that Sofia Ramirez is home sick today."

Addison felt sick too. "Oh, OK. Thanks," she managed to say. But inside, she thought, *What am I going to do?*

For the rest of the day, all Addison could think about was what would happen after school. When the bell rang, she was going to pick up Charlie from kindergarten like normal. Then she would have a choice to make.

Would she do the right thing and take her little brother home? Or would she take him to the playground alone instead and go to track practice?

I can't do that, she thought. *I really can't.*

It was one thing to have Sofia watch Charlie. It was an entirely other thing to have him play by himself.

But I would totally be able to see him the whole time, she thought.

But Mom would kill me, she thought.

She was still torn when she picked up Charlie that afternoon. As they walked, he was as happy as always. He went right into telling Addison all the kindergarten drama. Someone had gone to the principal's office and someone else had to go to the nurse.

Addison tried to listen, but she couldn't focus on her brother's words. When they got to the track, she knew it was time to make a decision.

"Where's Sofia?" Charlie asked, looking around the empty playground.

Addison stared at all the track athletes jogging out onto the field. Then she turned to her brother.

"Hey, Charlie," she said, "you know how you're always telling me that you're not a baby?"

"I'm not," her brother said.

"I know," Addison said. "And today you get to show me how big you really are."

She felt bad. But it would only be for one day. She would be able to see him the entire time.

Still, she couldn't shake the feeling she was doing the wrong thing.

"What do I have to do?" Charlie asked.

"All you have to do is play by yourself, here at the playground," Addison said. "I'll be on the field if you need me."

Charlie frowned. "All alone?" he asked. "Where's Sofia?"

"She's sick today," Addison said. "You'll only have to play for a little while."

"I guess I can do that," Charlie said. But he didn't sound sure. He kicked at a pebble with the toe of his shoe.

"Great! Thanks!" Addison said, already starting to jog away. "I'll be right over here, and don't talk to *anyone*, OK?"

"OK," Charlie said sadly.

During practice, Addison tried to concentrate. But she found herself looking over at her brother constantly. She even dropped the baton while practicing the relay handoff. She hadn't done that since the first practice. Ms. Barnes asked her twice if there was anything wrong, but Addison just shook her head.

Focus! Addison commanded herself.

But in the middle of a high-knee drill, she glanced over at Charlie again. He had his face pressed up against the chain-link fence that separated them. He looked sad and worried.

Addison gave a small wave and went back to lifting her knees. It was a struggle getting them high enough.

Usually, she felt amazing during track practice. But today, all she felt was shame.

When practice was over, Addison was totally exhausted—and relieved. She couldn't stand another moment of leaving Charlie by himself.

"See you all tomorrow morning! Remember, the activity bus leaves at eight o'clock sharp!" Ms. Barnes called as she dismissed them.

Addison barely heard the coach because she was already running over to the playground. Charlie was on the teeter-totter. He was trying unsuccessfully to make it work.

"Addie!" Charlie said when he saw her coming. "I think this thing is broken." He pointed at the teeter-totter.

Addison smiled. "You need two people to make it work," she explained.

Charlie looked up at her hopefully. "Can you show me how?"

Addison was tired, and all she wanted to do was go home. But she also felt bad for leaving Charlie alone. She wanted to make it up to him. "Of course," she said. "It's easy."

She sat down on the other end of the teeter-totter. Soon Charlie was howling with laughter as Addison bumped him up and down. His head bobbled and his little legs swung in the air.

"OK, buddy, we need to get home and eat some food," Addison said finally. She slid off her seat and lowered Charlie to the ground.

"Can we have ice cream for dinner?" Charlie said. Addison picked up both of their backpacks.

Why not, she thought. *He deserves something special for hanging out all by himself.*

"Sure," Addison said, grinning.

"Really?" Charlie's eyes went as round as saucers. Addison didn't think she'd ever seen him that happy.

"Yep," Addison said. "You can have all the ice cream you can eat." She ruffled his hair.

They made huge ice cream sundaes for dinner. They piled on the whipped cream and cherries. Addison even found some rainbow sprinkles. Charlie was thrilled.

"Thish ish amashing," Charlie said, his mouth full of ice cream. Chocolate dripped off his chin, and cherry juice was splattered on his T-shirt.

"It really is," Addison agreed.

They ate until their bellies bulged out. "Why don't you go watch cartoons while I clean up?" Addison said.

"This is the best night ever!" Charlie yelled. He ran into the living room and turned on the TV.

Addison cleaned up the sticky mess they had made. Her stomach was making strange sounds, and she felt slightly ill. Eating all that ice cream might not have been a great idea.

After she tidied up the kitchen, Addison watched the second half of a movie with Charlie. Then she put him to bed. Even though it was early, Addison crawled into bed too. She was tired from the long day.

Under her covers, Addison stared up at the ceiling. She was completely exhausted, but her eyes didn't want to close.

Her mind kept going back to the track meet tomorrow morning. It was all she could think about. *What am I going to tell Mom?*

CHAPTER 7

THE FIRST TRACK MEET

The next morning, Addison woke up early and stumbled into the kitchen. It was empty.

Where is everyone? she thought. Usually Charlie got up early on Saturday and camped out in front of the TV. Sometimes Mom even made pancakes with blueberries.

Addison poured herself some cereal and ate breakfast alone. Her stomach hurt, and she wasn't sure exactly why.

Was it because she'd eaten so much ice cream? Was it because she was nervous about the track meet today? Or was it because she was getting tired of sneaking around?

Addison sighed. She had another decision to make, and she had to make it fast. She could sneak out and write her mom a note, saying she was at Sofia's. Or she could be honest. She could tell her mom everything and hope she could still go to the meet.

Once Addison was done eating, she was still the only one awake. She decided to see where her family was. She went to Charlie's room and slowly opened the door.

Charlie was huddled under his blankets—and their mom was asleep on the floor. A bucket sat beside Charlie's bed. The room smelled like vomit.

Oh no! Addison thought. *Charlie must've gotten sick during the night. And it's my fault for letting him eat all of that ice cream.*

Addison looked at her mom. The dark circles under her eyes seemed even worse than usual. That decided it. She couldn't wake up Mom, who had clearly had a rough night. One more little lie wouldn't hurt.

I'll come clean about everything after the track meet, Addison silently promised as she went back to her room.

After throwing on her track uniform and running shoes, Addison stopped in the kitchen to write a note.

Hi, Mom! I'm going over to Sofia's house to work on a history project. I'll be back later this afternoon. Love, Addison.

There. That should do it. Her mom trusted Sofia and wouldn't question a thing.

Addison raced out the door and down the street to school. She just barely made the activity bus, but she had made it. She was on her way to her first-ever track and field meet.

Addison felt a rush of excitement and nerves when she stepped off the bus with the rest of the Bulldogs. They were on the Morrison Tigers track field. Hundreds of kids in bright-colored uniforms, all from different schools, filled the area.

Some of the kids were warming up with their teammates, doing jumping jacks and short sprints. Others were talking with their coaches or stretching in groups. The sun was shining brightly against the crisp blue sky. Addison fidgeted with the edge of her track uniform as she took it all in.

The Bulldogs found an area on the grass that was marked with their school name. The kids all dropped their bags and lunches into a heap.

Addison stood off to the side. She had forgotten to pack a lunch, or even a snack. She wished she could've told her mom about the meet. Mom would've made sure she had a lunch.

"All right everyone, let's do some warm-up laps!" Ms. Barnes shouted at the Bulldogs.

The kids got right to it. They started pulling off their sweatshirts. Addison tightened her old shoelaces one last time before heading to the track.

"Addison, the one hundred-meter dash is up first," Ms. Barnes said, walking over to her. "During your warm-up lap, make sure to get some sprints in too."

"OK, Ms. Barnes," Addison said. Her palms felt sweaty, and her skin felt hot. She couldn't believe she was going to run a real race.

The Bulldogs all ran together in a pack for their warm-up laps. Everyone was chatting and laughing.

But Addison ran at the back of the group, behind Brie, Ginny, and Laura. She wished she could feel as relaxed as they were. While she stretched out her legs, she couldn't help but think about all the things she'd been doing wrong lately.

She knew she shouldn't have left her brother with Sofia during track practice. She knew she shouldn't have let Charlie be alone the day before or let him eat all that junk for dinner. She knew she shouldn't be lying to her mom. Instead of her muscles loosening up, she felt tied in knots.

After a few laps, the Bulldogs and other teams cleared the track. The events would be starting soon. Addison stayed on the hard red gravel. It was time for her first race, the 100-meter dash.

"Good luck out there, Addison! You'll be amazing!" Brie yelled to her as she jogged away.

Addison gave a quick smile. She looked up at the stands that circled the track. They were filling up quickly with people. Addison stared at the sea of colors and felt that sick pit in her stomach again. Her mom and Charlie wouldn't be there to watch her first race.

"OK, girls, line up in your lanes!" a Tigers coach said into a bullhorn.

Six girls each took a separate lane. Addison was in the far right one. She glanced across at the other runners. Each girl had a fierce look on her face. Their fists were all balled up tight. Addison knew they wanted to win as much as she did.

The coach with the bullhorn yelled, "On your marks!"

Each girl lined her toes up precisely. Addison's heart was beating so hard, it felt like it was going to jump out of her chest.

"Get set!" the coach shouted.

Addison crouched down. She wiped her wet palms on her silky purple shorts. She looked up at the track. She could see the finish line. It was only a hundred meters away, but it felt like a million miles. Blood pounded in her ears.

BANG! The sound of the starting gun ripped through the air. Addison was off like a shot.

She had no more thoughts about Charlie, or Mom, or her own lies.

Her only focus was the finish tape and getting there first. Air rushed in and out of her lungs. Her feet hit the track. Her arms pumped. Her heart beat a steady, strong rhythm.

Addison didn't think about the other racers, or look around to see how they were doing. She only focused on her body. It knew exactly what to do.

In a little over thirteen seconds, the race was over. Addison looked down and saw the finish tape draped from her waist like a slim red belt. She had won!

The other sprinters gave her and each other high fives for running a good race. Addison grinned as she clutched her stomach and slowed her breathing. The pins and needles from her too-tight shoes began to lighten up.

Brie and Ginny rushed onto the track and wrapped her in a group hug.

"Nice job, Addie!" Ginny said.

Brie laughed. "See, I told you that you'd be awesome. Way to go!"

"Thank you!" Addison said breathlessly.

From the edge of the track Ms. Barnes gave her a thumbs-up and a smile.

Addison felt a bubble of pride fill her up. But then she looked into the stands of shouting spectators. That bubble popped, and all of Addison's mistakes came crashing back into her mind. Her throat grew tight. She wished her family could have seen her win. Charlie would've been jumping up and down. Her mom would've cheered. But they weren't there.

Addison went back to the Bulldogs' team area. The next few hours went by in a blur of starting guns, cheering crowds, and high fives. Addison tried to root for her teammates, but she couldn't get into it. All the excitement she had felt earlier seemed to have leaked out.

It was affecting her performance too. Addison lost the 200-meter dash to a girl from the Maxwell Lions. Addison could tell something was different right at the start. She hadn't felt the same freedom from before. Instead it felt as if she'd been running through thick mud.

Finally, it was time for the 4x400 relay race. It was one of the last events. Ginny lined up to take the first leg of the race. Brie, Laura, and Addison jogged in place to keep their muscles warm.

Addison lifted her knees high and pumped her arms. She wanted to focus on warm-ups. Maybe it would take her mind off everything else. She couldn't let her issues affect the team. After all, she was the anchor—the other girls were depending on Addison to give this race her best.

The runners took their position at the starting line. It was time to run.

BANG! The starting gun went off, and Ginny and the other girls launched into a sprint.

Addison cheered with the crowd as Ginny rounded the track. "Go, Ginny!" Addison yelled.

Ginny was out in front of the other five runners. She handed the baton off to Laura in a smooth motion. Laura raced away. Her long legs carried her down the track. Addison bounced on her toes as she watched to make sure her legs stayed nice and loose.

Laura was able to keep the lead during her lap. She passed the baton to Brie with a little wobble, and Brie slipped into second place behind a Lions runner. Brie's strides were powerful, but the gap between her and the other runner was widening.

In one more lap, it would be Addison's turn. She hoped she'd be able to make up the difference.

Before Addison knew it, Brie was headed down the straight stretch toward her. Addison held her hand out behind her, getting ready to start running. Brie's face was red and shiny. Addison could tell she was running out of steam.

The runner from the Lions' team came by first. Addison watched as the girl handed off the baton to their anchor. Brie was still ten meters away when Addison started jogging. She wanted to catch the other team.

From the side of the track, Ms. Barnes yelled, "Wait, Addison!" But it was too late. She was off.

Just as Brie drew near, Addison saw a flash of red out of the corner of her eye.

That's the same color as my mom's coat! Addison thought. She glanced over.

Sure enough, her mom was standing on the other side of the fence, holding Charlie's hand.

Addison forgot all about where she was and what she was supposed to be doing. Ms. Barnes' voice and her teammates' shouting blurred into the background.

She didn't hear Brie yelling, "Run, Addison!" She didn't feel the baton as Brie tried to press it into her palm.

She could only see the angry look on her mom's face.

There was a hollow clatter. The other runners flew past Addison as she realized her mistake. She looked at her empty hand. And then she looked down at the ground.

The baton was on the track.

I dropped the baton! she realized in horror.

Addison scrambled to pick it back up and started sprinting. But it was too late. The other runners were already halfway around the track, and there was no way she could catch them.

The Bulldogs were going to finish last. And it was all Addison's fault.

CHAPTER 8

IT ALL FALLS APART

That night, Addison lay on her bed and stared at the blue and red ribbons she'd received for the 100- and 200-meter races. She couldn't stop thinking about what had happened in the relay.

In her mind, she could see the disappointed looks on her teammates' faces. The Lions' team jumping and cheering after their runner crossed the finish line. Ms. Barnes hugging her and telling her that dropping the baton could happen to anyone.

And then facing her mom.

That was the worst part. Even worse than letting down her team.

It turned out that after Charlie had finished puking that morning, he'd told Mom everything. He'd told her about being at the playground all week with Sofia. About the ice cream for dinner. And worst of all, he'd told her about Addison leaving him alone at the playground the day before.

Addison's mom had been very angry, of course. So she'd called Sofia's house. But Addison wasn't there. The note was another lie. Sofia's mom got Sofia to confess that Addison was at the track meet. So Mom and Charlie had driven straight there.

Mom told Addison all of this on the drive home. Once they walked into the house, Mom had said, "I'm too angry to talk right now. Go to your room while I think about what to do."

So Addison was waiting.

She felt terrible. But she also felt like it wasn't all her fault. The lying was definitely her fault. But why did she have to be the one to always take care of Charlie? Why couldn't she join the track team? Why couldn't she have fun like every other kid?

Finally there was a knock at her door.

"Come in," Addison said, sitting up. Her mouth felt dry. She was so nervous.

Her mom poked her head in. "Can we talk?" she said. Her voice sounded surprisingly soft.

Right away, Addison began to cry. "I'm so sorry!" she sobbed.

"I know," Mom said. She sat down next to Addison on the bed. "I'm so disappointed in the choices you made. Especially when you left Charlie alone on the playground. That was very dangerous and very wrong. There are going to be consequences for that."

Addison nodded. "OK," she said with a sniff.

"But," Mom said, "I made a mistake too."

Addison looked up in surprise. "You did?" she asked.

Mom nodded. "I've been putting too much pressure on you."

"I just wish I could do normal kid things," Addison said, her tears turning into hiccups.

"I'm really trying," her mom said. "I'm really sorry. And I hope that next year you'll be able to join the track team. But we can't make it work this year."

Addison could just picture it. She'd be watching Charlie until she graduated from high school. Maybe even until she graduated from college. She'd never have fun. She'd never get to do anything after school besides come home and take care of her little brother. And she'd never get to be on the track team again.

She lay down and covered her face with her pillow. "Just go, Mom, OK?" Addison said. "I want to be alone right now."

A few moments later, she heard the click of her bedroom door as it closed shut.

CHAPTER 9

NEW SHOES

Addison quit the track team. For the next week, she did everything she was supposed to do. After school, she picked Charlie up from kindergarten. They walked home together, and Charlie told her everything that had happened that day. Addison made dinner. She cleaned up dinner. She put Charlie to bed. She did her homework. Then she went to bed.

And the next day, she did it all again.

On Thursday, as she and Charlie walked home from school, Addison glanced over at the track field. Laura, Brie, and Ginny were practicing baton handoffs. Another girl was there too. It looked like she had taken Addison's place on the relay team. Addison felt hot with jealousy.

Addison and Charlie continued walking. As they did, Addison couldn't help but think of what would've happened if she hadn't been distracted at the track meet. She imagined herself running. Brie slapping the baton firmly into her hand. Her legs driving herself forward with powerful speed. Her arms pumping back and forth. And her fingers gripping the baton so hard that there would be no way for it to drop.

"Ouch!" Charlie yelped. Addison had been gripping the baton in her imagination. In real life, she had been squeezing Charlie's hand.

"Oh, sorry, buddy," Addison said. "I was just daydreaming about running with a baton."

"You miss running a lot, huh?" Charlie asked, his big brown eyes looking up at her.

"Yeah, I guess," Addison said. She glanced back at the runners. "But I need to get over it," she added.

As Addison took one final look at the field, she noticed that Ms. Barnes was staring at her and Charlie. Addison quickly turned, and she and her brother walked away.

* * *

The next day after school, Addison waited outside of Charlie's kindergarten classroom feeling annoyed. She couldn't see Charlie anywhere. There were twenty other five-year-olds around her. They had sticky fingers, and they were all shouting, excited about the weekend.

Ms. Kathy, Charlie's teacher, waved at Addison. "Your mom picked up Charlie," the teacher said. "She said for you to meet her outside."

Addison wrinkled her forehead. "Oh, all right," she said. "Thanks."

Outside the school, Mom and Charlie were sitting together on a bench. As Addison walked over, she saw Ms. Barnes heading toward them. Addison felt a shiver of nerves. She hoped she wasn't still in trouble for all the track stuff.

Mom must've noticed the look on her face. "Everything's fine, Addie," she said. "Don't look so worried."

"What's going on?" Addison asked.

"Well, Ms. Barnes called me yesterday, and we had a long chat," her mom started. The two women grinned at each other as if they had a secret.

"OK . . . ," Addison said. She wished her mom would get to the point.

"Ms. Barnes told me how hard you worked on the track team," her mom continued. "She told me about what an amazing athlete you are."

Addison's cheeks felt hot. She didn't know if she was proud or embarrassed. Maybe both.

"And she had a really great idea," Mom said. "She told me that there's an after-school art program that might be great for Charlie. It's at the YMCA."

"Cool!" Charlie said. "I love art!"

Something like hope began to bloom slowly in Addison's chest. "Really?" she asked. "But can we afford it?"

"We can," Mom said. "They have special prices for single parents and those with, um, lower incomes. I talked to my boss, and I'll just need to shift my breaks a little so I can drive Charlie there after school. You'll pick him up after practice. And I'll drop you both off early at school in the morning. It's not going to be easy, but if we work together we can make it happen."

A grin spread across Addison's face. "I can't believe this," she said.

"There are details we'll need to figure out. Plus you're still grounded for leaving Charlie alone," her mom said. "But I think that you can join the track team. For real this time."

Ms. Barnes turned to Addison. "So are you ready to get your track gear on?"

"Oh, I didn't bring my things," Addison said, worried. She didn't want to miss another day.

Mom smiled and reached under the bench. She pulled out a duffel bag.

"I think I have something here that should work," she said.

"Thanks, Mom," Addison said. It felt good to be taken care of.

She took the bag, but it felt too heavy to hold just a pair of shorts and a T-shirt. She looked at Mom, who smiled back at her.

Addison unzipped the bag and let out a gasp. A shoebox was sitting on top of the clothes. "Really?" she whispered.

"Really," Mom said.

Addison opened the box. Inside were a pair of brand-new running shoes. They were bright pink with bits of yellow. It was like a neon rainbow.

Tears sprang to Addison's eyes. "Thank you, Mom," she said.

"You're welcome, Addie," Mom said. She stood up and brought her into a hug. "And thank you for all you've done for our family."

CHAPTER 10

RACE REDO

On the morning of Addison's second track meet, the sky was full of dark clouds ready to burst with rain. The air felt charged with energy as Addison jogged with her teammates to warm up for their relay race.

Suddenly fat drops of water burst from the sky. *This isn't good,* Addison thought, watching the rain pour onto the track. *What if the baton gets wet and slippery? What if I drop it again?*

She looked down at her bright pink running shoes and took a deep breath. They seemed to glow in the dark, misty weather. She wiggled her toes. She loved that she couldn't feel the ground through the soles. Her toes didn't pinch and hurt. It seemed like the shoes really were helping her run faster too. She'd already won the 100- and 200-meter races—this time by a landslide.

Addison had been able to practice every day for the last two weeks while Charlie went to the YMCA. She'd given track practice every ounce of her energy. She'd done all the extra drills. She'd sprinted until her legs could barely carry her home.

Her family's new schedule had been an adjustment. Not one of them liked early mornings. She and Charlie rolled into school grumpy and tired.

But it was all worth it. Charlie loved the YMCA and getting to play with friends. And Addison got to concentrate on being on the track team.

"All right, girls, time to line up," Ms. Barnes said. She wore a raincoat. The girls were in their track uniforms. Addison felt goose bumps dotting her arms as the rain hit her skin.

"It's slippery out there. Make sure your teammate really has that baton before you let go," Ms. Barnes said.

Brie squeezed Addison's hand. "We've got it down," Brie whispered to her.

Addison nodded. They'd practiced their handoff a million times.

Ginny got into the starting blocks, holding the yellow baton tightly in her right hand. The rain was coming down harder. It soaked Laura, Brie, and Addison. They linked arms to try to stay warm.

BANG!

The starting gun sounded, and the four different teams took off sprinting. Ginny had a strong start, but the Maxwell Lions runner quickly closed the distance. She took the lead.

In moments, Ginny was sprinting down the last one hundred meters, fighting her way through the rain. Laura stood ready with her left arm outstretched. Their handoff was picture perfect. Laura raced ahead, trying to catch the Lions.

"You got this, Laura!" Addison yelled. Everyone on the Bulldogs team was shouting too.

Laura was done in a flash. They were still in second, but Laura had shortened the gap as she passed the baton. Brie grabbed it and ran forward. Her arms and legs were a blur as she worked to catch up.

Addison's heart was pumping loudly in her ears, even though she wasn't running. It was almost her turn. She could already tell the last lap was going to be close.

As she waited, Addison quickly looked up into the stands. Sofia was there, and for once she wasn't reading a book. She put her hand up in a high five. Addison did the same, and they both smiled.

Next to Sofia, Addison could see her mom's bright red coat. Mom was cheering and waving her arms. Charlie stood beside her in his green raincoat. He was splashing in a puddle and probably getting very wet. They were both grinning at Addison.

This is it, Addison thought. Her family had made big changes just so she could run. She wanted to make them proud.

Brie came flying around the last corner. The Bulldogs were still in second place, but the third-place Eagles runner was gaining on Brie. Addison wanted to start jogging forward, but she knew that it was too soon.

The Lions girl who'd beaten Addison at the 200-meter dash in the first meet was anchoring for her team. She stood next to Addison, hand out and ready. She was really fast, and she would have a head start. Addison knew that this wasn't going to be an easy lap.

Brie was almost to her now. Just at the right moment, Addison started to jog, stretching her arm behind her. Brie reached and reached and then *slap!*

The baton smacked into Addison's hand. Her fingers wrapped around it. There was no way she was letting go of the baton.

Addison took off. Her new shoes slapped the track, splashing small puddles of water. But she didn't notice the rain anymore. She just ran.

Her arms pumped. The muscles in her legs felt strong and sure from all of the extra conditioning exercises she had done at practice. She thought that she might be the fastest girl out there. She just needed to show everyone.

Addison left the third- and fourth-place girls far behind. But the Lions girl was harder to catch. She was running a great race. As they came around the last corner, Addison and the Lions runner were neck and neck.

Addison could hear the rest of the Bulldogs cheering for her over the rain. Through all the noise, she heard Charlie's unmistakable voice yelling, "GO, ADDIE!"

Addison felt a surge of power. She could see the red finish line tape through the fog and rain. Her legs went faster and faster. And then, just at the last second, Addison bolted ahead of the other girl.

The ribbon broke around her hips. Laura, Brie, and Ginny rushed around her, jumping and shouting. Addison couldn't tell if she was crying or if it was just rain rolling down her cheeks.

Addison looked up at the stands. Sofia was cheering. Charlie was too, and so was her mom.

With the rain pouring down and everyone cheering, Addison had never felt happier.

ABOUT the AUTHOR

Joelle Wisler is a freelance writer and physical therapist. She's written several sports stories, including the Jake Maddox JV Girls books *Spinning Away* and *Beyond Basketball*. She grew up in South Dakota and is a lifelong runner, jumper, bender, and skier. She spends much of her time these days laughing at her husband and chasing her two kids around—and any stray moose that might wander into her backyard in the mountains of Colorado.

GLOSSARY

anchor (ANG-kuhr)—a member of a relay team who competes last

baton (buh-TON)—a hollow rod that is passed from one runner to the next during a relay race

concentrate (KAHN-suhn-trayt)—to put your full focus and attention on something

disqualify (dis-KWAHL-uh-fye)—to prevent someone from taking part in an activity; athletes can be disqualified for breaking the rules of their sport

drill (DRIL)—a repetitive exercise that helps you learn a specific skill

lane (LAYN)—a narrow part of a track that is used by a single runner during part or all of a race

meet (MEET)—a sporting event featuring many races or contests

sprint (SPRINT)—to run fast for a short distance

starting blocks (STAR-ting BLOKS)—a device that supports a runner's feet at the start of a race

stride (STRIDE)—a long step

tape (TAYP)—a string stretched across the finish line that is broken by the first person to cross the line

DISCUSSION QUESTIONS

1. Describe Addison's personality. Do you think she usually keeps secrets from her mom, or is it out of character for her? Talk about it!

2. In Chapter 6, Charlie agrees to play by himself at the playground while Addison is at track practice. Discuss how you think he feels about being alone. Use examples from the story to support your answer.

3. Why do you think the author titled the book *Back on Track*? How does it relate to the story? Brainstorm other title ideas that would also work well.

WRITING PROMPTS

1. The climax is the most intense part of a story. Often the main character has to face his or her problems. Write a paragraph about which moment you think is the climax. Be sure to explain your reasoning.

2. Addison decides to join track without telling her mom. Using examples from the text, write two paragraphs that describe how keeping this secret affects Addison throughout the story.

3. Imagine you're friends with Addison. Write a letter to her that suggests ways Addison can follow her running dreams—without lying to her mom.

MORE ABOUT
TRACK AND FIELD

Outside of the United States, track and field events are called *athletics*. Track events consist of running and hurdling. Field events involve throwing and jumping.

Track and field is one of the oldest organized sports. It can be traced back to 776 BC, when the first Olympic Games were held in Greece. Only men were allowed to participate, and the original Games had just one event—a 600-foot race called the stadion. Eventually, more races and other events were added.

Although the first modern Olympics were held in 1896, women's athletics weren't added until 1928. The only events at the time were the 100-meter race and 4x100-meter relay.

A runner's time cannot be counted as a world record if the wind is pushing against her back at more than 4.5 miles per hour. The strong gusts can give the runner a speed boost and an unfair advantage.

The record holder of the 100-meter dash is often called the fastest man or woman in the world. American Florence Griffith Joyner, nicknamed Flo-Jo by fans, set the women's record in 1988 with a time of 10.49 seconds. Jamaican Usain Bolt holds the men's record, finishing the race in 9.58 seconds in a 2009 competition.

The women's 4x400-meter relay record is held by the USSR with a time of 3 minutes and 15.17 seconds, set in the 1988 Seoul Olympics. It was a close race. The U.S. team crossed the finish line just 0.34 seconds after the USSR.

American sprinter Allyson Felix is the only female track athlete to have won six Olympic gold medals. Her events include the 200-meter race, 4x100-meter relay, and 4x400-meter relay.

THE FUN DOESN'T STOP HERE!

FIND MORE AT:
CAPSTONEKIDS.COM

Authors and Illustrators | Videos and Contests
Games and Puzzles | Heroes and Villains

Find cool websites and
more books like this one at
www.facthound.com

Just type in the Book ID:
9781496575364
and you're ready to go!